I0683898

Sunrise on the Porch

Dale P. Rhodes, Sr.

Jan-Carol
Publishing, Inc
"every story needs a book"

Sunrise on the Porch
Backyard Adventure Series
Dale P. Rhodes, Sr.
Published September 2022
Skippy Creek
Imprint of Jan-Carol Publishing, Inc.
All rights reserved
Copyright © Dale P. Rhodes, Sr.
Cover Art and Interior Illustrations: Brenden Stakem

ISBN: 978-1-954978-58-4
Library of Congress Control Number: 2022945846

Jan-Carol Publishing, Inc.
PO Box 701
Johnson City, TN 37605
publisher@jancarolpublishing.com
www.jancarolpublishing.com

I would like to dedicate this book to the many loved ones, both people and pets, who are no longer with me. I thank God for the times I have shared and the memories that I hold on to. Smiles, laughs, voices and sayings, hugs and kisses, barks and meows, and purrs and tail wags are the things I count most dear in my life. I believe that we should never miss an opportunity to let our loved ones know how we feel about them, so to my family and friends and pets, please know that I love you.

Author's Note

There are blessings that are so valuable they are without price. Love and friendship give us strength to endure the hardships of this life and make the good things so much better. Wisdom can help us make better choices. Faith in God can be the difference when all else fails.

Sunrise on the Porch

Leo, a 15-year-old hound dog, is awakened by the footsteps of his human walking down the hallway. Looking up with a sleepy eye, he sees his human looking back down and smiling.

"It's time to wake up, old friend. I have to go to work today, so I have to ask you to stay outside." The human speaks softly as he pets Leo's head and gives a gentle tug on his collar.

Leo begins to slowly move, rocking himself back and forth to get momentum enough to stand up.

Waiting patiently, the human speaks again. "I see you are a little stiff this morning. That's okay, I am too," he says, bending over to help Leo up onto his feet.

Leo is never quite sure what the human is saying, but he really likes the help up. Standing steady once more, Leo slowly moves towards the door. The human holds the door open and with a little pat on the side, Leo steps out the door and into the darkness. Out into the yard he goes to make sure everything is safe for himself and his human. And of course, to do all the other things a dog must do early in the morning.

After a little while, Leo completes his trip around the yard and makes his way back to the porch. The soft glow of string lights overhead gives him just enough sight to make it to his water bowl. Slowly, he lowers his head to take a drink when suddenly he is startled by a deep "BOO" from inside the bowl.

"Owwlll," Leo howls, as he takes a terrified step back.

The water splashes as Leo's bullfrog friend, Bronson, lunges to the surface and rests his arms on the rim of the water bowl. "Good morning, my friend." Bronson says, with a deep rumbling laugh.

"You get me every time, Bronson," Leo says, panting from the scare and then leaning in beside Bronson to take his much needed drink of water. "You've been scaring me for a long time, my friend."

"Yes I have, or have you been pretending to be scared?" Bronson asks.

Raising his head up from the water bowl after having his drink, Leo thinks for a moment of all the times that Bronson has scared him over the years and then replies, smiling, "Well, there have been a few times when I have pretended to be scared, but today you really got me, friend."

Bronson smiles at the thought of having fun with his friend Leo. The two friends sit and talk for a while longer under the soft glow of the string lights as the sky around them slowly begins to become less and less dark.

Leo looks up to notice that the lights have gone out. "Sunrise will be here soon my friend. What have you planned for your day? Perhaps a swim in the lake at the back of the woods?" he asks.

"Oh, I don't know if I'm ready for that yet," Bronson says nervously.

"Well, you just remember that God has given you everything you need to be an excellent swimmer. All you have to do is jump," Leo encourages.

"I know, I know. One day I will surprise you," Bronson promises.

"I believe you will, my friend," Leo says.

As the next few moments unwind, the sound of many birds chirping fills the air. A red bird couple, Reuben and Ruby, lands on the porch banister, singing as they do. "Good morning, good morning. It's such a lovely day."

"Good morning Mr. and Mrs. Redbird. How are you this fine morning?" Leo asks with a hopeful look on his face, as he does every morning. "Is perhaps today the day you begin to build your new, bigger nest to make room for some little ones?"

"No. Not today, Mr. Leo," Ruby answers, trying not to look sad, Reuben holding her close.

Leo softly replies, in his most comforting voice. "Not to worry, dear couple. You hold on a little longer. The Lord knows your dreams of having children and I believe it will happen at just the right time."

"Thank you for the encouragement, dear friend," Reuben says, with a smile.

Just as Reuben is smiling, footsteps can be heard above them in the tree branches and coming down the tree at the corner of the porch. Landing on the banister, a little out of breath, Sedona, a female squirrel, comes to a quick stop. "It's almost time. Is everyone ready?"

"Yes it is, and how are you this morning, Sedona?" Leo asks, glad to see the excitement in her eyes. "What are your plans for the day? Possibly a grand adventure to a far away place where you will make new friends?"

Shaking her head, Sedona replies, "No, not today, I have too much work to do. I am still filling my tree with acorns for the winter."

A warm orange glow comes up in the distance, and everyone's eyes open wide. This is what they have been waiting for.

Leo's human is about to open the door when he sees through the glass that Leo has friends watching the sunrise with him, so he pauses to wait it out. Quietly he motions for the other humans in the house, and they all come to the window to see the gathering on the porch. No one says a word for the next few moments, not the humans and not Leo and his friends. The sun slowly rises above the horizon, and then the orange glow is gone and replaced with a giant orange ball in the sky.

Leo and his friends all look around at one another and say, "This is the day which the Lord has made. We will rejoice and be glad in it."

As they all stand to their feet, Sedona looks over to Leo and asks, "What are you gonna do today, Leo?"

Leo takes a tired breath and says, "I don't feel just right this morning, so I think I will rest here on the porch for a while longer."

All at once his friends reply, "We can stay here with you."

"Thank you," he says. "But no. You all go and have adventures and come back tonight and share wonderful stories with me."

With his word of blessing they all go their own way for the day to enjoy the plans they had made. The house door opens now and

Leo's three little sisters, Maybell, Lucy, and Bella, come flying by to get to the yard to do their business. Being alone now on the porch, Leo lays his head down on his legs to rest. Just as he begins to settle into his thoughts, the little ones jump back onto the porch. Sniffing around in a frantic craze. They can smell Leo's friends.

"Okay girls, let's get you back into the house," the human calls out as he holds the door open again.

Hurriedly, each one passes by Leo, stopping only briefly to sniff and bump noses with him and then run into the house.

As they all step into the house, Leo begins to smile. He thinks back to the time that Bronson first met the little ones. It was another day, very much like today but several years ago. The sun was shining. The air was warm but not hot. There was a soft breeze. In fact, it really was a perfect day. He was laying on the porch and Bronson was relaxing in his water bowl. They raised their heads and looked at each other when they heard the sound of many footsteps on the other side of the door. Neither one knew what the sound was but they both soon found out. The door opened and three little dogs ran out. Their little feet moved faster than Leo thought possible. Out the door they came and down the steps and out into the yard. It seemed as though they had never seen green grass before. They ran and ran and ran. Around the yard and back and forth. Chasing one another and just running to be running.

Suddenly, Bella spotted something and stopped. She began to sniff the ground and started walking around sniffing. Then, she started digging faster and faster. As if she was looking for something.

Maybell and Lucy decide that rolling on the grass on their backs was the right thing to do at that moment. Twisting this way and that, as if they needed to scratch an awful itch.

Bella stopped digging because she was hot and out of breath. She stood there panting.

Lucy had found some tall grass to chew on and Maybell just laid still in the sun on her back.

Walking slowly to the porch, Bella decided she'd had enough digging. When she reached the porch, she headed straight for the water bowl. Not seeing Bronson in the bowl, Bella jumped in to cool her feet and the wave threw Bronson out the other side.

Bronson landed with a splash right in front of Leo.

Shaking off the water, Leo began to laugh at what had happened.

Bronson was surprised by the whole thing and tried to quickly get himself together, which made Leo laugh even more.

Seeing that Leo's friends have all left, Leo's human comes back out onto the porch, as he is heading out to work for the day. He stops to say goodbye to Leo as he always does. "I have to go to work ol' friend, so you be a good boy, have a good day, and remember, I love you," he says, holding Leo's chin in his hands and resting his forehead against Leo's for just a moment before he goes his way.

Leo spends his morning resting and thinking of the wonderful things his friends must be doing and the life he has at the house as he drifts off to sleep.

Mid-afternoon comes, and the sun rays have shifted direction and are now coming over Leo's shoulder. He lays still on the porch, awake but still not feeling well. He counts the day as a good one because he has so many friends to spend time with, and he thanks God for his wonderful life.

Thoughts of his brothers and sister who have all gone on to Heaven flood his mind. He has missed them for quite awhile. He remembers the times they had growing up running and playing and even fighting sometimes, but they always had each other.

Leo has something to tell all of his friends, but knows it will be something they won't want to hear. He has thought about it for days now and can't seem to find the strength to bring it up. Lying on the porch seems to be the only thing he does have strength for, but it's time for him to make another trip out to the yard.

He really didn't want to walk around the yard, but he is glad that he has come. The breeze blowing in the grass brings so many smells that he loves. The human that lives next door has been baking all morning and he wishes he could have a taste. The pine tree forest down the road is always wonderful. The flower garden in the backyard never disappoints.

Slowly Leo makes his journey around the yard and heads back for the comfort of the porch. His pillow is still there waiting for him when he returns. Laying down proves to be no easier than standing up and Leo moans a little from the stiffness and pain as he does. Finally being settled into place brings a sigh of relief.

Sleep comes again for Leo as the afternoon sun warms his back. Dreams overtake him and rest is good. He feels young again, if only for a little while.

Nap time comes to a close with the splashing of water from Leo's bowl. Bronson has returned from his days activity and wants to relax for awhile.

"I'm sorry, old friend, I didn't mean to wake you," Bronson apologizes.

"That's okay," Leo says, rubbing his eyes. "I've been looking forward to everyone getting back so you can tell me about your day."

"Well I had a pretty good day, if I do say so myself," Bronson boasts.

15

"I am so glad to hear that," Leo replies, excited to hear the story.

"I did what you said, old friend. I went down to the lake," Bronson proclaims.

Leo's ears perk up. "You did? Oh my word, I wish I could have been there! Did you jump in?" he asks, excitedly.

"No," Bronson confesses. "But I did meet some other frogs, so maybe next time."

"Wow. I'm so happy for you. You'll be splashing around in the lake in no time."

Bronson begins to blush a little as he says, "Well, it's only because of you, old friend. You just wouldn't let me forget about that dream."

"I believe in you, my friend, and I want you to be happy," Leo says.

A happy melody fills the air, and Leo and Bronson look at each other and at the same time say, "Reuben and Ruby." Smiling in anticipation they both turn to the porch rail as the Redbird couple swoops in and lands.

"You two seem to be in a good mood," Bronson says with a smile.

"You sure do," Leo adds. "Are you having a good day?"

"We are. We've been gathering twigs for a new nest," Reuben says.

With his eyes now wide open, Leo asks, "Does this mean you two are expecting little ones soon?"

"No, not exactly," Ruby explains. "We have decided to trust God to fill the new nest with little ones, so we figure we should go ahead and build it."

"That is excellent! I'm so happy to hear that," Leo says with an ever widening smile.

"Yeah, guys, way to go," adds Bronson and starts splashing in the water bowl to make everyone laugh.

Before all the water stops splashing, everyone notices the sound of footsteps in the tree limbs above them. They all look up to see

Sedona zigging and zagging from tree to tree until she reaches the porch. "Hey everybody," she says very excitedly.

They all reply at once. "Hi Sedona!"

"You guys are not gonna believe what just happened to me," she continues on without a breath.

"What happened, Sedona? Are you alright?" Leo asks.

"Yeah, I'm fine," she says.

"Well, what's going on then?" Bronson asks, looking just as puzzled as everyone else.

"Okay, so, I went out to gather acorns and such for my store for winter, and I kept going out farther and farther from the yard. After a while, I decided to take a break from working and just go running from limb to limb," Sedona continues.

"You do that all the time," Leo comments, wondering what's coming next in her story.

"I know, right?" Sedona agrees. "But this time as I'm climbing and running and jumping and climbing, I jump from one tree to another as fast as I can when out of no where, I'm hit and start falling."

"Oh my!" Ruby says, hanging on Sedona's every word.

"I know! Crazy, right?" Sedona asks.

"So what did you do?" Bronson questions.

Finally taking a breath, Sedona finishes the story. "It turns out that the thing that hit me was another squirrel. He was running through the tree tops like me, except from another direction. He side swiped me and we both started falling, our arms and legs flailing, trying to grab hold to a limb before we hit the ground."

Sedona's friends are all shocked, with their eyes and mouth wide open. After a brief pause they all ask, "What happened next?"

"Well," she says, pausing for dramatic effect. "Once we both stopped falling, we figured out what happened and had a good laugh. He told me he lives on the other side of the forrest and was out hunting for food as well."

With a big smile on his face, Leo says, "Sounds like you have made a new friend."

"I guess so, yeah!" Sedona replies. "We have decided to hunt for food together until we both have enough for winter."

"Well, that sounds like fun," says Bronson.

"It certainly does," agrees Reuben.

"I feel much better knowing you have a friend to help you now," says Ruby.

🐾 🐾 🐾

As everyone continues on chatting, Leo begins to realize that all of his friends have had a wonderful day and he feels very good about what they all have done. He thinks to himself that this may be the only time that he can tell them his news. This is something that he has thought about for a while, but could never muster enough courage to talk to them. It breaks his heart to know that it will spoil this wonderful day, but it must be done and if not now, when?

He let's them continue on talking for a little while, enjoying their company. Watching their faces light up as they tell their stories. Memorizing their voices. Loving them all.

Finally, Leo decides it is time to have the talk with his friends, so he clears his throat, which is something he rarely does. Everyone gets quiet and turns to look at him, suddenly realizing that all is not right. "I need to tell you all something," he says softly.

With a serious voice, Bronson responds, "What's wrong, old friend? You know you can tell us anything."

To that, everyone else adds, "Yes of course. What is it?"

"It's not easy to say and you won't want to hear it, but I believe it is true." Leo says, his voice breaking up. He pauses for a moment while he takes a deep breath to regain his composure.

Everyone begins to look even more worried at what he is about to say.

"I told you that I didn't feel well this morning. Truth is I haven't felt well for some time now," He says, softly.

"That's okay, we will all pray for you," Sedona says reassuringly, and the others join in her thoughts by nodding their heads.

"I love you all for that, but I believe it is my time to go," Leo says as he lowers his head, not really wanting to look them in the face.

"Go where?" Sedona asks, but really she already knows.

Bronson speaks up. "You mean, time for the Lord to take you home to Heaven?"

"Yes, old friend, that's exactly what I mean," Leo answers.

"Oh my," Ruby says, not sure what else to say.

"Are you sure?" Reuben asks, quietly.

"Yes, I believe so."

"NOOOO! It just can't be. You'll get better!" Sedona cries out, tears streaming down her face.

"It's okay, Sedona. It's going to be okay," Leo soothes her.

Everyone turns to look at him, tears now flowing from all of their faces. Silence fills the porch and seems to spill over into the whole yard.

Leo breaks the silence with what he hopes will be comforting words. "I never understood these kind of comments when I was younger and the older ones would say them to me, but I can tell you even though it is difficult to think of leaving you all, it seems like it is the right thing. I have a peace inside that tells me it's okay. I can see that it will be hard for you all to accept, and I understand that, but please let's not spend the afternoon discussing this. Let's just be together. Please tell me your stories of today's adventures one more time."

Everyone gathered around Leo and began again to tell their stories, and when they finished they thought of other stories to tell him. He loved every word and the feeling of all of his friends being with him. Sometime during the warm afternoon, Leo drifted off to sleep one last time and the angels came and carried his spirit away to heaven.

Everyone continues talking and laughing until Sedona notices how quiet Leo is. "Hey guys, I think Leo is asleep. Maybe we should go, so we don't wake him."

Turning to focus on him more closely, Bronson discovers the truth. "No, dear," he says in his deep voice as comforting as he knows how. "He's not asleep. He's gone. He was right. The angels have taken him away to Heaven."

"NO! NO! It can't be!" Sedona cries frantically as she begins pushing on him. "Wake up, Leo. Wake up," she begs, now sobbing with tears pouring from her eyes.

"Sweetheart, it's too late. He's not here," Ruby says, trying to help her understand.

Still crying, Sedona hugs Leo's neck and answers. "But I don't want him to go. I love him."

"We all do. None of us want him to be gone, dear," Reuben says, softly patting her back.

"We will see him again one day, Sedona," Bronson adds, reminding her of the hope they have to help them to feel better.

Everyone holds close to Leo and each other and just cries for awhile.

The sound of crying is soon overcome by the sound of a car engine, and Leo's friends all look up to see what it is.

Leo's human has come home from work and is parking his truck. Just like any other day, he gets out and walks toward the porch. Looking up onto the porch he finds it odd that Leo's friends are all sitting close even as he walks up. Just as he reaches the steps they all slowly back away from Leo. Now Leo's human knows that something is terribly wrong. He looks at Leo and then his friends.

"Leo, are you alright, boy? Wake up. I'm home." He calls out, hoping to see Leo wake and be happy to see him.

Looking once again over to Leo's friends, he sees all of their sad faces and knows that Leo has died. Sitting down beside him, he holds him tightly and begins to cry.

Leo's friends sit and watch with amazement. They have never seen Leo's human cry.

A long time passes and finally Leo's human stands up again. He turns to go into the house, when he sees Leo's friends still sitting there. He pauses for a moment and looks straight at them. After speaking to them words that they cannot understand, he begins to cry again and walks into the house.

"Do you know what he just said to us?" Sedona asks.

"No, but it sounded okay," Bronson says.

"We will watch him through the window and see what he does," Reuben says.

"Great idea, honey, I'll take this one and you take that one," Ruby says, pointing to a window on the other side of the porch as she flies into place.

They watch the human as he goes through the house. He goes out another door at the back of the house and then into the shed out in the yard. Everyone watches him walk around the house and down the hill a little.

He stops somewhat close to the beautiful tree that they all look at every morning as the sun rises. There he lays one of the tools down and starts digging into the ground with the other. Sometimes he switches tools but continues digging and digging. No one says a word. They just keep watching. After a long while has passed, the human stops. The hole he is digging is very big by now and he seems very tired.

The human walks back to his house, up the porch steps and inside. He comes out moments later with Leo's blanket. He carefully wraps Leo inside the blanket and carries him down to bury him by the big tree. The other humans come out and they all talk and cry for a while before they finish with the burial. One by one they all return to the house.

Leo's friends notice over the next few days how sad his human is. He goes out to work and comes back home with the same tired look on his face.

Leo's friends are sad too. The whole yard is very quiet every day. They still meet every morning on the porch, but without Leo they don't feel the same excitement for the day.

Day after day goes by, pretty much the same as the day before. Everyone does the same things as they always do, but no one seems to want to anymore.

Then one day, Leo's friends notice that something has changed. There is a different feeling in the air. There is music coming from Leo's house again. Something they have not heard in many days. Leo's human walks out of the house and to the shed again. He comes out moments later with tools in his hands and heads toward the big tree in the yard again. This time he starts to dig on the other side of the tree from where he buried Leo.

Bronson and the others watch with puzzled looks on their faces.

"Why is he digging another hole?" Sedona asks.

"Very strange," Ruby comments.

"I've never seen a human do anything like this," adds Reuben.

Shaking his head, Bronson says, "Well, Leo loved him, so let's just wait and see. Maybe he will surprise us."

The friends all sit on the porch and continue to watch as the human continues to dig. He digs for hours. The hole gets wider and deeper as the time goes by. When he is done digging he brings a small wagon that he pulls behind his tractor. He loads the dirt into the wagon and takes it far down in the backyard and dumps it out. When all of the dirt is moved, he stops for the day.

Every weekend the human continues to work on his new project. Once he is finishes digging his hole, he begins something else. He brings out lumber and other tools.

The friends gather together every time he works to watch and try to figure out what on earth he is doing. Once in awhile the red bird couple will fly overhead to watch him a little better. Sometimes, Sedona will hide in the tree above him.

Measuring and cutting and nailing and painting, the human stays very busy. One day he leaves in his truck and when he returns he has plants in the back. Flowers and bushes and tall grasses, and he plants all of them around the large hole he has dug by the big tree. The next day he brings a tall pole out of his shed that had a wooden box on the top of it. He digs another, smaller hole and puts the end of the long pole in the ground with the wooden box sticking up high in the air.

Next he brings out a smaller wooden box and attaches it high in the big tree.

The next day, Leo's friends hear the rumbling sound of big trucks rolling up the driveway and stopping near the yard. Leo's human is back out working on his project. The first truck drops off some big stones which the human moves one by one and places around the big hole in the ground. The next truck backs up close to the big tree. It's driver gets out and stretches a hose over to the big hole. He opens a valve and water begins to flow from the hose to the hole beside the tree.

"The human has lost his mind now, I think," says Sedona as she and the others watch the flurry of activities.

"What do you think, Bronson? Why is the human filling the hole with water?" Reuben asks.

Without taking his eyes off of the tree and the hole and the human, Bronson just shakes his head. "I honestly don't know what he's doing."

Soon the big hole is full of water and the large truck leaves. Now the only sound in the yard is that of the human as he continues to work. Placing plants and stones until he feels they are just right. Next he goes back to his shed and comes out with a fountain which he puts in the center of the hole of water. When he turns it on it shoots water up into the air and makes a beautiful, relaxing sound.

"Is that what I think it is?" Sedona asks, with a puzzled look on her face as she watches the human finishing his work.

"It certainly does look like one," Reuben confirms.

"I didn't know he could make one of those," Ruby adds.

"Leo used to say that his human could make lots of things, but I wonder if he knew that he could make a pond?" Bronson says as they all look on in amazement.

The human puts away all of his tools and then comes back and just stands and stares at his work. He looks from one side. Then he moves to another spot and looks some more. And then from another spot. Next the human begins to smile and starts to whistle as he walks back toward the house.

The group of friends all sit quietly as he continues to move toward the porch, hoping that he will not notice them. As he gets closer they realize that he is looking straight at them. No one knows what to do, so they all do nothing. And then it happens. Something none of them would ever have expected.

He stops right in front of them and slowly bends down and picks up Bronson. The others are in shock and simply watch to see what will happen. Bronson is scared stiff and freezes in the human's hand. The human lifts himself up and holds Bronson face to face. Then he smiles and rubs Bronson on the head. Looking down at the others he motions for them to follow him and he walks down toward the new pond with Bronson in his hands.

Sedona, Ruby, and Reuben all just look at each other for a moment and shrug their shoulders. Then they follow the human to see what he wants.

When the human arrives at the new pond, he says something to Bronson and then bends down and gently places him near some stones.

Then he pats him on the head again and smiles. Turning towards the others he motions again for them to follow him and he walks over and stands in between the pole and the tree.

The others again look at each other and then move toward the human. The red bird couple look closer at the box on top of the pole and notice that it is a huge bird house with many rooms. They fly up together to check it out.

When Sedona sees them fly into the bird house she turns to look at the tree and realizes that the human has made a house for her as well. So, she climbs up to look inside.

After a few moments, all of the friends meet on the ground at the edge of the pond.

"I had no idea that he was making us all new homes," Ruby says.

"I know. Isn't it wonderful?" asks Reuben.

"Yes it is. We are going to have room for lots of little ones!" Ruby adds.

"You certainly will," Bronson agrees, "and we all have a beautiful pond to enjoy."

"Hey, Bronson, was the human talking to you when he put you back on the ground?" Sedona asks.

"Yes. I have no idea what he said, but it sounded very much like what he used to say to Leo. And Leo seemed to always like hearing it, so I do too."

Sedona is filling her new house with acorns.

Ruby and Reuben are making plans for little ones in their new house.

Bronson is loving the new pond. He thinks of Leo every time he jumps in and is glad he is no longer afraid.

And every weekend the human watches the sun rise from the porch and watches over Leo's friends as well. He also brings Maybell, Lucy, and Bella out to watch the sun rise with him. They mostly just run around the yard, but maybe one day they will sit and watch.

The End

Acknowledgments

Thank you, Lord, for all the loved ones in my life.

About the Author

Dale P. Rhodes, Sr. has lived in Central Virginia his entire life. He enjoys music, sports (go Miami Dolphins), movies, his pets, and spending time with family. Writing was a secret hobby growing up that came back to him as he watched his father suffer with Dementia. Beginning with poetry, he has moved into Christian fiction, and is currently working on the third book in his *City on a Hill Series*. *Sunrise on the Porch* is the third book in his *Backyard Adventure Series* and Rhodes is excited to one day share the entire series with his three beautiful granddaughters, Delphina, Isla, and Sophia.

About the Illustrator

Brenden Stakem is a student at Savannah College of Art and Design, and is currently majoring in 2D Animation with a minor in Sequential Art. He enjoys designing and concepting characters, and hopes to one day work for a professional studio to bring those characters to life. You can find more of his work on Twitter (@purplestakes) or by visiting purplestakes.wixsite.com/home.